I0639498

John Skirrow Peart

Christmas day and other poems

John Skirrow Peart

Christmas day and other poems

ISBN/EAN: 9783743384729

Manufactured in Europe, USA, Canada, Australia, Japa

Cover: Foto ©Andreas Hilbeck / pixelio.de

Manufactured and distributed by brebook publishing software
(www.brebook.com)

John Skirrow Peart

Christmas day and other poems

CHRISTMAS DAY

And other Poems.

BY

JOHN SKIRROW PEART.

ALL RIGHTS RESERVED.

LONDON:
SIMPKIN, MARSHALL, & CO.

1871.

LONDON:

W. H. AND L. COLLINGRIDGE, CITY PRESS,

ALDERSGATE STREET, E.C.

PREFACE.

IN submitting this little volume to the public, it is with the hope that, if all be not acceptable, some stray thought or expression may be found to give both pleasure and profit. The poem "Christmas Day" is an attempt to describe what Christmas Day is to nearly every man, woman, and child in England—a laughing, happy time. So far the poem is a national one. The religious phase of our great festival has often been set forth in verse, but what may be called the worldly one never, except in a passing line or two. If it fail to recommend itself to the reader, may I be pardoned the failure in the respect for the motive. If it be successful, and a desire should be felt to know whether the description be a true one, I say, ask the Vicar or the Squire.

J. S. P.

January, 1871.

TO THE

REV. WILLIAM FIDDIAN PEART, M.A.,

VICAR OF MYTHOLMROYD,

THE FOLLOWING POEM IS DEDICATED

AS A TOKEN OF AFFECTION AND RESPECT

BY HIS NEPHEW,

THE AUTHOR.

CHRISTMAS DAY.

'Tis Christmas time, the snow lies on the
    ground,
The wind blows chilly from the northern sky.
A village Squire's mansion may be found,
Snug in the hills not far from Banbury;
The well-built walls the biting blasts defy,
And all is comfortable, bright within.
Its lord—a polished gentleman is he.
Dissenters though he owns amongst his kin,
Yet doubting Church and State, is to him mortal
    sin.

The household meet to share the morning meal :
The father in the pride of forty-four ;
The mother's lovely face does yet reveal
Its girlhood's beauty, tho' now near two-score ;
The daughter, Helen, some fifteen or more,
Displays to all a maiden's little airs ;
The younger ones throw Robin crumbs, or bore
Big, patient Pompey, or talk play affairs :
God bless those happy hearts, their day will come
     for cares !

The grandame joins.   Those venerable hairs
Deck the calm forehead with a silver splendour ;
That chaste expression on the face she wears
Which only years and simple faith can lend her.
How often we impatient service render
To age, the link between us and the grave !
Then let us towards them be more patient, tender :
Our being, health, was it not they who gave ?
Our children will to us, as we to age behave.

The Postman's ring!   Away the youngsters fly,

To seize the bag, and bring it to the table;

The father knows his power and dignity,

And looks as weighty as he well is able.

He feels inclined to foist some little fable;

But seeing all their glad expectancy,

His kind heart will not brook a moment's trouble;

So he announces, pleased as pleased can be,

"Bertie and Tom from school, and Charlie home

    from sea."

Then wild the mirth. The mother's happy smiles

Full well the flutter in her heart attest;

Though tender love for all her bairns she feels,

Charlie's the scapegrace, so she loves him best.

The servants share the pleasure with the rest,

Have fits of laughter, yet they know not why;

By some keen thinker, tho', it may be guessed

That thoughts of sweethearts are not far away;

The Squire's word being pledged for early holiday.

They gather round the fire on Christmas Eve :

Charlie amongst the children bears the palm ;

And homage as his right he does receive,

Both from his heirship and his uniform.

He talks of wonderful escapes from storm ;

Of "jolly larks " enjoyed when free on shore ;

And should an enemy invading come,

With patriot fervour does that foe implore

As British midshipman, to let him know before.

The Rugby boys have much whereof to speak :

How Doctor Hayman, simple truth to tell,

Knows more of caning than he does of Greek ;

How Bully Smith had thrashed Tom's chum,
      Roupell ;

How Tom had fought till Bully conquered fell,

And how the Tutor said, " 'Twas very wrong,

Still, to be just, Tom used his mauleys well."

Then cricket, boating, on the memory throng :

Tales such as ever will to schoolboy days belong.

The others listen with a proud delight,

The grandame nods her head with meaning
  wise,

As if to say, that, should she please, she might

Tell still more startling feats of enterprise;

The parents' swelling hearts transported rise,

As silently they watch the happy brood;

Each thinking of their offspring's destinies,

A holy breathing wings its way to God—

" Give them all other things, but make, O make
  them good! "

The morning breaks—the natal morn of Christ:

As one by one the family appear,

From tongue to tongue that greeting old is
  passed—

" A Merry Christmas and a glad New Year."

The father bids them in remembrance bear

Their many mercies, when compared with
  those

Who have no home, no bread, and scant to wear;
Think of the bitter wind, the drifting snows,
Then weigh their own blest lot—warm shelter,
    food, and clothes.

Once more the Postman shows his welcome face,
Then Christmas Cards are opened with a will;
My favourite Helen gets some good advice,
She's bid "Heap on more wood, the wind is
    chill;"
The picture shows a redbreast on a hill—
Robin ten times the size the hill should be!
But children are not always critical;
And notes inviting their society
At gatherings of all kinds, till past Epiphany.

Now to the village church they all resort,
Whose spire, the sentinel of centuries,
Points, like the precepts old beneath it taught,
Unerringly and calmly towards the skies.*

---

* See note A at the end of this volume.

The ivy screens the time-stained buttresses,
To lend antiquity a softer glory ;
Death counts his conquests by the mounds that
    rise,
Marking the resting-place of young and hoary :
Most have a cross, or stone, to guard their memory.

May I in some such quiet spot be laid
When my last work is done.   Let me not have ·
A stiff, cold marble reared above my head,
But let a yew-tree grace my humble grave.
Far rather there than in a stately nave,
Where Honour keeps dull vigils o'er Renown ;
No such distinguished burial I crave.
My requiem be the song-bird's dulcet tone,
And childhood's happy laugh, wild in its sporting
    grown.

The villagers are loitering round the gate,
And greet the manor party with a smile,

Perhaps more pleasant for the next day's treat.

All enter reverently the cloistered aisle ;

The glorious service echoes through the pile ;

Communion succeeds the Litany :

The Curate then announces from the rail

That " all the parish will expected be

To-morrow at the Squire's for dancing, and for

    tea."

The agèd Vicar now the desk ascends :

Time but small havoc with his frame has

    made,

A vigour rare his eighty years attends ;

And like the ancient monarch of the glade,

Yet upright stands, majestic though decayed,

And waits the tempest that shall lay him low ;

So he, for death nor eager nor afraid,

Serenely to the Master's will doth bow ;

He fears not for the past, to come — God will

    bestow.

A simple sermon his :—" We meet this day

To celebrate the Saviour's birth—His praise

Is hymned where winter holds eternal sway,

And where the sun his fiercest might displays.

Wide are the tongues in which his loved ones

    raise

Their Alleluias : black, white, rich, or poor,

Jesus to all an equal heeding pays ;

The song's the same from London's busy

    roar,

As the uncertain note from Patagonia's shore.

" Does trouble weigh you down ?   Go, ask His

    aid ;

He shall accord it ere you form the prayer :

Has sickness caused the hopes of years to

    fade ?

No hand like His to smooth the bed of care :

Is wealth your blessing ?   Then to Him repair,

To seek direction for its useful spending :

Is poverty's affliction hard to bear?

Beneath the same our Lord on earth was
  bending:

You never can be wrong, on Him for help de-
  pending.

" Has one of you a fault still unconfessed?

Has one of you a foe still unforgiven?

Before you go, assoil the laden breast;

Let anger from your heart by love be driven;

Our Lord forgave till seventy times and seven;

The Evil one's temptations must be borne,

These are the pitfalls on the road to heaven;

Remember, if within them you be drawn,

You add to Calvary's wreath another cruel thorn.

" I've tried Him long, and always found Him
  true—

True as the needle to the distant pole;

Not doubtfully I preach this faith to you,

Within a stone's throw of my earthly goal:

Full soon the bell of this old church will toll

My passing hence to joys untold above,

That distance far Conception's weak control;

My parting prayer is, that you all may prove

The first, last, surest good, to be the Master's

    love.

" How sweet to mark to-day's reunion

Of scattered families! This surely may

Prefigure that foretold communion,

When all Emmanuel's mandates shall obey.

The emblem, too, of blest eternity.

And now, belovèd flock, for many an hour

Go raise the merry dance and roundelay;

Be prosperous your lot, content your store,

And may the Lord be with you now and ever-

    more."

When home again, arrivals follow fast;

The Squire beaming greets them at the door;

First, comes the white-haired clergyman to cas

An apostolic tone on the affair ;

Next, a self-satisfied and portly pair,

The authors of three pretty, budding lasses,

And many more, whose tale I must forbear;

Instead, here is a sum for Rugby classes—

Join youth and mistletoe, the answer will be—

     kisses.

They spend the daylight on the manor pool :

The elders romp till they feel young again—

Unconsciously confirm the Bible rule,—

The spirit dies not, though the body wane.

To use some gallant aid the maidens deign ;

Then, silly girls ! shriek in affected tones ;

Loud laughter meets their falls, and shams of

     pain,—

No nostrum like a laugh for bruisèd bones ;

Old Christmas is sworn foe, to bigots, prudes, and

     —groans.

The dinner bell! If animals wrote books,

How they would damn our blest festivity!

Goodwill to men; to cows, pigs, fowl, and rooks,

A Saint Bartholomew of butchery.

The Jewish priesthood, too, were wondrous free,

In sacrificial frame, at letting blood.

The Squire's table was a sight to see;

All was abundant and old-English. Would

That all my country's poor had such substantial food!

Now for the good old game of blind-man's buff;

The men the girls hold longer than they need:

Of course it is from dread of being rough

That hands so tenderly on cheeks are laid;

Then do the nimble feet the dances speed—

The "Lancers" and the grand "de Coverley"

Then by the willing mother 'tis decreed,

To please the bantlings, that the Christmas-tree

Be stripped—when each one gets what will least

useful be.

Oh Youth, how blest thy portion! Thine the
    time
When what to men seems worthless still can
    please;
Ere long simplicity will blush, a crime
In thine eyes and the world's. Now prompt to
    seize
Enjoyment's passing moment. O sweet Ease!—
No care for future, careless of the past;
All ignorant of Fortune's strange decrees.
Pleasure her motto at thy feet hath cast—
Enjoy, enjoy to-day, to-morrow cometh fast!

The ocean volume rolls with gloomy roar
Unlike the tributary of the field;—
The streamlet cannot float the ship of war.
The oak-tree doth his rising sapling shield:
The sapling can no strength for vessels yield.
So Care from Innocence will stand aside;

Not far away, but just his shape concealed,

Awaiting calmly Passion's certain tide;

Then claim his ripened prey, nor will he be denied.

The grandame marks all with delighted face,

Already has three matches in her eye;

Tho' knowing times have altered for the worse,

She's loth to judge with due severity.

Then treacherous thought along the past doth

    fly,

And opes again her long-closed girlhood's home;

From there, through forward years full rapidly,

She kneels beside her mate's far-distant tomb;

She checks a falling tear, of hope, I ween, not

    gloom.

Old Christmas has to answer for a deal

Of heart-disease as well as happiness;

.Beneath the mistletoe how many feel

Tho blush of love's first bashful ecstasies!

Together picture, oh, such matchless bliss!

In which papas and portions have no share;

Soon to be dashed by servile prejudice:

Must we our idol from the bosom tear?

No; though the shrine be sealed, the first love's
ever there.

'Tis two o'clock, and time the scene should
close,

For even Christmas joys must have an end;

The servants wait to lead them to repose:

The Vicar solemnly the knee doth bend,

And prays—that happiness may each attend

From purer source than earthly: lest they
fall

The grace divine may plenteously descend,

And keep them ready for their heavenward
call;

Then rising, spreads his hands, and says, "God
bless you all!"

Before those holly-boughs are taken down,

The busy world will thread its busy way

Of thought and carefulness again to crown

A year of toil with well-earned holiday.

Long hold this festival a rightful sway—

That in its blessings equally may share,

The sons of Want and of Prosperity.

And now, perhaps, the Squire will grant my
prayer,

That he next Christmas-time invite me to be
there.

STRONG DRINK.*

If Parliament should read this rhyme—
The thought is impudence sublime:
   *   *   *   *   *
           So I won't ax 'em.—Ver. 17.

THE pride of Scotland stooped to sing,

In words with genius glistering,

Encomiums demonstrating

        The joys of drink ;

Forgot how many at that spring,

       Young, ruined, sink.

---

* See note B at the end of this volume.

I'll tell thee, though in humbler verse,
Of its insidious, hidden curse,
That hurried me from bad to worse
           In rapid flight:
There's ruin both to soul and purse
                     In " getting tight."

Some call it venial—any name
But that which is its right one—shame;
They say, " We must not strongly blame
                     The faults of youth ! "
Oh, habit in the man's the same,
                     I've learned that truth.

My cheek runs hot as I confess,
That my first cup was called—excess ;*
The quaffing of the draught was bliss,
                     Its dregs remorse;
Long, long, 'twill be ere I shall miss
                     Its baleful force.

---

* For this expression, "That my first cup was called excess," I am indebted to J. B. Gough, Esq., the Temperance Lecturer.

What is there in the fiendish skill
That tricks my palate 'gainst my will,
That leads me on from fill to fill,
   From more to more?
Each time a bottle nearer hell
   Than that before.

'Tis not for me—the social glass
An hour with pipe and friend to pass;
And—just to oil our intercourse—
   A nip of grog;
A lord of God's great universe
   Chained like a dog!

There's, maybe, pleasure in the wine,
For when half-drunk you're half-divine;
Song, Music, Painting—all the Nine,*
   Are at your call;
Then drop from angels down to swine
   In one swift fall.

---

* See note C at the end of this volume.

Next morning, "just to put you square,

Of that which bit you take a hair : "

So it goes on from year to year,

　　　　　Until death come.

Tipsy at Judgment !　Can ye hear

　　　　　Your righteous doom ?

Yet, ah ! Reflection won't be quelled !

The retrospect of hopes dispelled

No agony has e'er excelled

　　　　　In depth of pain ;

But by that gripe demoniac held,

　　　　　You writhe in vain.

You promise nothing shall you force

To seek again that fertile source

Of fault, sin, sorrow, and remorse ;

　　　　　You swear by oath.

What comes of promise, vow ?　Of course,

　　　　　You break them both.

All wrong! all wrong!   That fatal thirst
Ye cannot ultimately worst;
And so I counsel from the first—
   Reserve your mettle.
No pugilist but Jesus Christ
   Can thrash a bottle.

Those chords in every human heart,
Which make us God's own counterpart;
That quiver with convulsive start
   At sorrow's pine;
Ecstatic thrill at some sweet thought
   From source divine :—·

The charm of Love's pure, gentle sway,
The surest guard in youth's wild way,
Of manhood's heart the faithful stay,
   When tempests lower;
The light that lends new brilliancy
   To pleasure's hour :—

The sense elastic that the Spring,

The Summer—different seasons bring,

Alike for peasant and for king,

         The mossy brink,

The wood—wide nature's following :—

         All dulled by drink.

Or when the eager mind would fain

Burst this flesh prison, and attain

Those fancy realms of gorgeous sheen,

         Of song's renown;

Why hang a bottle on the brain

         To drag it down?

Who cares with senses steeped in wine,

" To see the rose and woodbine twine ";

To cull the scented gems that line

         The mountain path ?

May such delights be always mine

         On this side death : --

(If Parliament should read this rhyme—

·The thought is impudence sublime—

They'll stop my walks in right quick time ;

    So I won't ax 'em ;

They'll find the hills I love to climb,

    And then—they'll tax 'em.)

And aye hereafter ! This my pleasure—

To roam the heavenly scenes at leisure,

And there to con my darling treasure,

    A simple song ;

The bliss above I cannot measure

    If that be wrong :—

O blest reunion !   Once again

To see departed loved ones.   Then

And ever with them to remain

    Through blissful hours ;

Each passing moment to attain

    Some nobler powers :—

To talk of long-past times, when we

Together stemmed life's heavy sea;

When trouble's surging seemed to be

        No moment lighter;

There's nought like pain and poverty

        To make Heaven brighter:

To know, to hear " the mighty dead,"

Those who have writ, those who have bled,

To twine around their country's head

        A deathless glory;

Whose sacred names are registered

        In many a story :—

And last, not least of Heaven's reward

That, there will be, my trusted Lord,

Whom I have served and whom adored

        But small at best,

Familiar friend! as well as God—

        Thought must the rest!

With me it was the death of prayer;

When laden with a weight of care,

I would to God's great throne repair,

   My want confessing ;

With brain afire, how could I dare

   To ask a blessing?

Yes, Man, in God's own image made!

In immortality arrayed!

To whom the right of angels' grade

   Is freely given,

Will let a bottle barricade

   His way to heaven !

A felon raves in that cold cell,

Oh, pity him !   He knows full well

There's not an hour 'twixt him and hell,

   For evermair ;

Can ye not hear his frenzied yell

   Of dark despair?

C

There stands a man on Thames' side—
Or from despondency or pride
He cannot God's command abide,
       For his long home ;
So leaps into the rolling tide,
       To snatch his doom.

Poor Perdita walks every street,
With aching heart and aching feet,
She seeks maybe some safe retreat,
       And gets—"For shame !"
But thinks hereafter she may meet
       Those virtuous same :—

A wife forsaken yonder lies,
Hearing her babe's beseeching cries
For bread, bread, bread ; away she flies
       For him to steal ;
Nature breaks Honesty's last ties,
       But brings a meal.

Yes! thousands are their woes bewailing,

Either through theirs or others' failing;

Of most (how many lack detailing?)

    Strong drink's the devil;

Who'll nerve his right arm for assailing

    This blasting evil?

I can't quite reach the Royal ear,

At present mine's a humbler sphere,

So I'll address my cousins dear—

    The Parliament;

And ask them cordially to bear

    A compliment!

Your Legislation, each one knows,

From deeply-pious feeling flows;

Yet some may venture to suppose

    You're not quite blameless:

Let me a thing or two disclose,

    Which I call shameless.

There's something in the liquor laws—
Vic. I., cap. 10, the millionth clause—
(But here I think 'tis best to pause

        My legal lore :

Lest you create me—with good cause—

        Lord Chancellor).

You've everywhere an institution
To breed theft, murder, prostitution,
And spread abroad that destitution

        Which you bewail;

So, then, by way of restitution,

        You build a jail.

With one hand pay a preaching parson,
The other feeds a crime—say arson ;
Thus far you've helped the monstrous farce on

        In generous halves ;

Till cleverly you've set one class on

        At t'other's calves.

I really cannot help but wonder

That you and rogues remain asunder;

But, no! you turn with looks of thunder,

   Rejoice you've caught 'em.

You feel no mercy for their blunder,

   And yet you've taught 'em.

Bob Lowe should take one by the hand

With gratitude, and say, " Dear friend,

The liquor money this year's grand,

   I thank you kindly;

You've scattered wealth thro' this great land,

   Though maybe blindly.

" You'll go to gaol—you've been before;

On coming out, go, drink some more;

Our schools stretch thro' from shore to shore,

   From north to south;

The richest taxes that I score

   Go through your mouth."

Shame, crying shame ! that cruel flout,
The senseless, mad, triumphal shout,
When told the balance brought about
>> For *small* requitals ;
That revenue is torn from out
>> Old England's vitals !

Shame, crying shame ! a " Christian " nation
Should cherish her inebriation ;
Should hold, for swift and sure repletion,
>> Of wasting purse,
That source of revenue, damnation,
>> And England's curse.

O Britain ! highly-favoured land,
Strong by the Sea-god's mighty hand,
Thy laws obeyed on every strand,
>> Great is thy power !
Prouder than Gaul or Allèmand,
>> Thou art yet lower.

Let me thy son, with tender care,

A parent's fatal failing bare,

Though its destruction mayhap tear

> Thy frame with rigour,

Yet soon thy future shall repair

> That needful vigour.

Dear isle of Freedom! Why endure

A vice which must ere long ensure

Thy fall? When, lo! thou hast the cure

> In thine own grasp;

Then, Britain, turn from its impure,

> Its loathsome clasp.

Are not thy children faithful? Where

Is the high people that shall dare

A step on England's sacred shore

> With hostile tread?

Thy living sons their blood will pour,

> Like those long dead.

No foreign foe thy cliffs shall breast;
But in thy borders stalks a pest
That vitiates the strongest, best,
   Of thy life's blood.
Oh, battle with it! and the rest
   Leave thou to God.

They call thee Albion, blest of heaven.
Much is required, if much be given;
When from thy soil this stain be driven,
   Fair shalt thou rise;
Nobler, that thou hast nobly striven
   For what is wise.

Thy sons are great; but canst thou guess
How many of them through excess,
That doth all noble aims depress,
   Are lost to fame?
Will England future ages bless,
   Or hug her shame?

'Tis said all nations bow to thee
In wealth, art, science, poesy,
In pity and in liberty,
   In high command;
Wilt thou in pureness backward be,
   My native land?

And if religion form the crown,
Wider shall spread thy wide renown,
Until, from pure to perfect grown,
   Jesus descending
Shall claim thee as His cherished own,
   World without ending.

ROLANDO.

When first I bid farewell to England's shore,

And on Atlantic billows westward bore,

I fondly thought in other realms to find

Some happier spot than that I left behind.

As the lone traveller on Sahara's strand,

Wearied and thirsty, toiling o'er the sand,

Some fancied haven far ahead descries,

He strives to reach it, but the vision flies.

The earth seemed brighter, and the flowers more
      fair,

When viewed through novelty's deceptive glare;

The cascade's music and the warbler's strain

More sweet when wafted from a distant main.

Such are the idle dreams of youthful years,
Though gloomy now, the future bright appears ;
The lessons taught by sages gone before—
Youth's wiser now than old men were of yore !
Life, like a landscape on a summer's day,
Has sober tints commingled with the gay ;
Thus pain and joy alternately are given ;
One tells of Earth, the other speaks of Heaven.
Youth see the sunshine, not the darker shade,
Laugh at the errors which their fathers made,
Till, by the same experience taught, they rise
To dear-bought wisdom, and in turn advise.

Mine's been a restless life, a life of care,
Few friends to comfort and no love to share ;
Through many a land, by love of moving
        sped,
Rolando's Arab foot has marked its tread.
And yet, methinks, a life is better spent
In gaining knowledge than on riches bent.

The business man, who has no thoughts be-
    yond
His ledger, balance, or his goods in bond;
The office drudge, within whose narrow mind
A row of figures, and no more, we find;
The struggling lawyer, poring over books
As faded as his weary-hearted looks;—
Shall it be said that these fulfil the end
Of noble life, yet others be condemned?
The man who lives for self, and self alone,
Denies his destiny, vacates his throne.

For self alone! I mark that quiet form
Thread yon close alley's uninviting gloom;
An angel he, though in man's humbler guise,
To ease, if not to banish, miseries:
Vice, Destitution, reign in triumph there,
Disease, dirt, dissolution, charge the air.
Some faces yet refinement's ruin show,
Others suspicion keen, or vacant woe.

They all have seen Humanity's dark phase—
How few have turned its brighter to their gaze!
I mark him as he treads that weary bourne,
Bestows a flower whence he plucks a thorn,
Contrives to drop some useful lesson, while
He calls the long-forgotten, banished smile.
Nothing too hard for him—the lost, sick, dying,—
Not one he leaves without a balm supplying.
Yes! threadbare tho' he be, unknown his name,
I'd rather have his lot than wealth or fame.

Ye rich, ye great, whom luxury surrounds—
In whose abodes unthinking mirth resounds,
Draw but the curtains of your noble halls,
And listen to Despair's heartrending calls.
Take from the trappings of your needless state,
For those who bend beneath Want's crushing
    weight;
The blessing of mankind? a priceless treasure!
But ease is dearly bought with God's displeasure.

Mark ye the blackness of the nearing storm?

Can ye not see grim Revolution's form?

Have ye not felt aught of the smouldering fire

Beneath you?   Does not Cowardice inspire,

If Justice will not, some relenting deed?

Or is fatality your impious creed?

Mark Discontent approach with angry eyes,

The strong-defiant greater strength defies.

Hunger and Right have often asked their own;

Instead, as to a dog, you threw a bone.

But now, with Resolution in the van,

They come again.   Refuse them if ye can

Or dare!   That word once spoken — then the
        last,

Brief, day of toleration will be past.

How'long will legislation count it due

To grind the many to exalt the few?

Reversing Nature's law—the law Divine—

And then stand wondering at pale decline.

But have the few impetuous seemed to aim
At right unquestioned to exalted name
By laws beneficent, by lives unstained?
Alas for faith! faith human in mankind.

Two rulers pledge two nations: these we call
William, Napoleon, Germania, Gaul.
Solemn their coronation oaths! They swear,
By all the powers of Heaven, Earth, and Air,
Never to violate a people's faith,
But keep it sacred till absolved by death.
Tramp, tramp, tramp, tramp! resounds the martial
     train—
Squadrons on squadrons close, yield, close again—
The Rhine runs blood, and corpses strew the
     plain.
Fair France's fertile fields of grain are shorn;
Her orchards—deserts; villages forlorn.
A starving, bleeding peasantry appears,
Content—at discount for a hundred years!

And why? lest perjured pride should have a fall,

A hundred thousand slaughters were too small.

Thus did a patriot flame these rulers grace!

Noble example from exalted place!

The one, to bolster tyranny a day;

The other, hoary baby, just to play

A silly hour as Kaiser—then decay.

Mark ye the laden vessels leave our shore,

(Succeeding months extend the number more)

Freighted with what the dullest mind must own

The very life of England—her backbone.

The labourer, the artisan, must leave

His native country, hopefully to strive

In some more thankful land for daily bread,

A humble roof to shield his honest head.

Industrious, finds here no room for toil,

He plants his bitterness in foreign soil.

He takes his tools, his skill, his strength, his all;

Once gone, that wealth is over past recall,

D

And thinks of England only as the place

Where crime or starving stared him in the face.

The mother spurns the offspring from her breast,

Then whines of duty, love, and all the rest!

And thousands more less fortunate than those

Who have no means to leave behind their woes.

The only remedy, our statesmen say,

For starving is—to ship the starved away!

A remedy! 'tis treason better called!

A crime against the commonwealth!   Behold

The fields extensive, stretching through the land,

Asking small labour of the planter's hand

In all the lavishness of wealth to smile:

Seek there the cause of Industry's exile.

The few's injustice keeps these wide preserves;

The pheasant fattens while the peasant starves:

Demand a piece, out comes the entail scroll,

Which holds for ages what the Norman stole.

Dead Cobden, rise! and shake the senate hall,

Till this iniquity shall totter—fall!

Turn we from effete systems to a spot
No monarch envies, envious though its lot.
Its wealth—simplicity, its strength—its sons,
Its poverty—its soil. And yet there reigns
Contentment—happiness.   No exile train
Winds through those defiles for a richer main.
While Justice stays, so rich and yet so poor,
Shall Swisserland's small domain stand secure.

For self alone! stay yet a time with me,
While, by the occult power of poesy,
I call some witnesses. Though bare those walls—
Though no reflex from gilded carving falls
In splendour round me—yet they shall appear.
But hush! attend! the "famous dead" are near!

" Helvetia writhed in Austria's iron grasp,
And all but yielded to his hated clasp.
The point which pierced base Gessler's tyrant heart
Was but despairing Virtue's last resort.

My native country, mistress of my soul!

Thou gav'st my life, it was at thy control!

With eagles cradled my first breath was drawn

In Freedom's eyrie—slaves were ne'er so born.

Life without liberty was death to me:

A mountain nursling ever must be free.

I pressed upon my rocks a sacred kiss,

And vowed no tyrant e'er should make them
     his.

Those rocks, to others wretchèd, barren, cold,

Were fairer far to me than burnished gold.

The heart clings always where the treasure is—

My treasure was my country's happiness.

And now I go, Magician, fare thee well,

Thou know'st the name I bear is WILLIAM TELL!"

  "No genius was mine; that altar flame

Shed no refulgence round JOHN HOWARD's name:

Yet, without influence or genius, may

An earnest worker benefit his day.

To some is given the power to wake the soul

To ecstasy; to others, the control

Of senates, or a nation's destinies:

My proper sphere was humbler far than these.

I know my life by many, hard, was viewed,—

Oh, no! there's 'luxury in doing good.'

And yet I did but turn the opening sod

Of that long road where many since have trod

With equal ardour.   I now hear men say

No scope is left for wide philanthropy:

Wrong! wrong! the love of race is ever wide,

And scope for every creature is supplied;

God never yet gave being to a man

But what He marked for him some useful

    plan.

Hear me, ye listeners—but seek, ye'll find

A work for every one, of every kind.

And, now, who comes?—farewell!—let him be

    heard—

'Tis DAVID LIVINGSTONE awaits thy word!

"They stamped my work as useless—waste of
    time
And strength—hypocrisy—nay, almost crime,
To take the sextant, and to leave the school,
Some said, enthusiast, and others, fool.
The multitude discerns not future good.
They only ask, ' Will this bring money ? food ? '
A noble few were willing to believe
That the long warp might yet the woof receive.
A pioneer first must tread the way
For civil good and Christianity.
Then let them say I struck for world-wide fame ;
To me is now as one their praise or blame.
How long will man with others interfere ?
Fix his hereafter, when they've damned him here ?
Or when will all accept this simple creed—
That conscience, God, or both, may prompt the
    deed ?
None ever yet accomplished lasting good
Who fearful of the world's decision stood.

Rouse me no more, O man! I must away,

For spirits have their work as well as clay."*

  A blest reflection! When life nears its close,

When duty done has earned its long repose,

When age's locks and furrows give the face

A beauty rarer than all manhood's grace;

When early friends have nearly passed away,

And only youth reminds us of to-day—

That the long road has not been trod in vain,

But deathless footprints in our track remain.

Soft be the dust whereon he lays his head,

And blessings hang like incense round the dead;

While those who courage have "to do and dare"

Learn, like Elisha, then the mantle wear.

  But in succeeding numbers let me dwell

On countries soon; of differing peoples tell.

Perhaps some worthy lesson I may teach;

Perchance some deeply-rooted error reach;

---

* See note E at the end of this volume.

Some folly that in greater freedom grows,

Disguised in Reason's drapery, disclose.

If this be so, imperfect though the strain,

I rest content—my words have not been vain.

Columbia, then, must first a notice claim,

Carving with eager hand a mighty name;

And if the Maker's bounty can insure

A nation's might, Columbia shall endure.

There Strength the man, while Beauty is the bride,

To sum her charms in one—Creation's pride.

Show me but one who ne'er has felt the power

Of Nature's beauties in some pensive hour;

Her sterner page to noble aims inspire,

Her tempest moods fan Resolution's fire,

Her gentler features often to impart

That happy sadness which refines the heart.

If such an one there be, then is his soul

Dark as the grave, and frigid as the pole.

Her sturdy children, in the eager race

For earthly greatness, hold a forward place ;

High in design and urgent to attain,

They scorn discomfort, while they laugh at pain.

And whether found on the Antarctic strand,

Braving the dangers of an unknown land,

By Niger's flood, or on the mystic Nile,

They bear the impress of their mother isle.

Had it not been that England's deeds are theirs,

That our great teachers schooled their rising
       years,

Columbia had rushed to wild excesses,

Or quickly sunk in luxury's caresses.

Cradled in wealth, their failings are not those

That the rough blasts of poverty disclose ;

But rather such as insolently tower

In the proud livery of conscious power ;

For, like a wayward child, too early freed

From master's discipline, or mother's heed,

They revel in their freedom newly gained;
Their mien is haughty, but their wisdom feigned.

Already may be felt throughout the land,
The urgent need of some strong pruning hand.
The harmless decoration of a name,
The homage which exalted titles claim;
These are desired, now Wealth and Power unite
To gild the structure, dazzle vulgar sight;
While Education's pride delights to show
That legislative power degrades the low.
The nation's wisdom rests not with the wise,
Her early dignity, uncared-for, flies.
These evils, gathering vigour from neglect,
May slowly spread, but none the less infect;
Until a despot rise, and with the sword
Scourge, till a humbled people own him lord.

'Tis but a while, Columbia, bowed with grief,
Wept o'er the body of her murdered chief:

A pall of mourning hung around the land,

Deep was her sorrow, paralyzed her hand.

The murderer's ruthless stroke that laid him low

Wreathed but enduring glory round his brow :

The cruel hope which urged that fatal aim,

But crowned a patriot's with a martyr's fame ;

And in a nation's heart his memory stored

A fond but sad possession. Then record

This simple story over his remains :

" His fated hand destroyed the bondman's
   chains."

No pompous sculpture o'er his burial frown,

Leave the approach a portal of renown.

In future years the noble and the brave

Shall drop a grateful tear on LINCOLN's grave.

 O Liberty, thou " fairest of the fair,"

Let me thy laureate's proud title bear :

My soul, impatient, speeds the strong desire ;

Bestow the boon, and then the words inspire.

Borne round the earth on Fancy's active wing,
The dirge of woe I chant, or bliss I sing.

In different realms, behold a monarch's state,
Surrounded by a people's silent hate :
The helpless prisoner for no crime atones,
And martial music drowns despairing groans.

Behold the noble's arrogant display,
To scorn the source of his prosperity ;
An angry scowl pervades the peasant's eye,
As his more happy brother passes by ;
Perhaps a new-led bride, a daughter fair—
His fondest treasure—hope of many a prayer—
Is snatched to gratify the brute desire
Of some base wretch whom love can ne'er inspire,
And vain the wronged one should the wrong unfold,
When Justice smothers Conscience under gold.

Behold the slave, with heaven-directed face,
Implore a curse on his oppressor's race ;

From him e'en Hope, that fond deceiver, flies,

As round his future darkening horrors rise :

Forgive him, then, if, maddened by his woes,

He grasp the sword, and spring upon his foes.

Methinks I hear, from many a child of pain,

The echo of the patriarch's complain :

" Accursèd be the day when I was born ;

Let Death's dark shadow stain its future dawn ;

Let awful blackness o'er its passage loom,

Nor light nor sound relieve the angry gloom.

Say, why doth life its tedious periods roll

O'er him who groans in bitterness of soul ?

Oh ! wherefore when I left my mother's womb

Did I not sink into a ready tomb ?

Tho only haven by no storm opprest ;

Tho wicked cease from troubling there, the weary

      are at rest."

Thus fare the realms beneath tyrannic sway ;

Now brighter prospects beckon me away,

And as a bird from northern rigours bound,
The distance past where Winter pales the
    ground
Alights awhile on some dividing plain,
Where lingering Summer owns disputed reign,
To bask delighted in the sunbeams' play,
And trim his feathers ere he hold his way;
So linger I, my sullied pinions plume,
Breathe new existence, and my course resume.

   Yes, Liberty! where thou art wont to dwell
A myriad blessings thine attendance swell,
Far richer good thy magic presence yields
Than famed Alpheus on Arcadian fields.
Thou great Protectress, in thy circling arms
Exulting Genius, free from mean alarms,
Throws grateful vigour into works sublime,
And leaves unfading monuments for time.
And who like thee to touch the hidden spring
Which prompts the sacrificial offering

Of wealth, home, comfort—saving honour,—all,

At a loved fatherland's unrivalled call?

To-day despotic power, wherever seen,

Turns pale at thy approach. Ere long, I ween,

The swarthy Saracen shall welcome thee,

And the slow Othman wake activity;

Thy benefits on Libyan plains descend,

And Brama's offspring thy great shade defend.

And as the Maker with almighty skill

Impressed a perfect beauty on His will;—

Not only made the matchless orb of day,

But, to give finish to His mastery,

Put forth the moon with her more gentle light,

That each by contrast might be more complete;—

So thou, O Liberty! to be more blest,

Take thy sedater sister to thy breast:

Freedom and Faith, be thy joint flag unfurled,

A twin effulgence sway a willing world.

MAGDALEN'S APPEAL.*

The ship is ready; ere a day be past,

My fatherland will vanish from my sight;

The scene of both my happiness and woe.

But, as I leave, I cast upon the shore

My hapless tale, and breathe to Heaven a prayer.

In one of England's fairest villages

My father's peaceful rectory was seen;

And every Sunday in the dear old church

Whose spire was bent as with declining age,

And cast its shade o'er centuries of dead,

He preached of love to Christ and love to man.

Of how our blessed Lord no sinner spurned,

But said to penitents, "Go, sin no more."

How He rebuked the vaunting Pharisee,

But justified the humble Publican ;

And taught the noble lesson that we ought

To lean to mercy when another falls.

My long-lost home!   The honeysuckle twined

Around its porch, dispensing fragrance there,

The foretaste of the happiness within.

And in the garden, where with childish glee

I gambolled with the neighbouring noble's son,

Bloomed   England's   floral   brilliants — Passion

　　flowers,

The Laurestinus, and the sweet Moss-rose.

I knew them all, their every name and place ;

But strangers tend, and strangers pluck them now.

An only child was I, my parents' hope ;

The burden of full many a pious prayer.

And with what care they watched and shielded me,

From all the influence of worldly pride,

Those who have loved an only child can tell.

Methinks that angels circled that abode,

Which caught its tone from heavenly intercourse.

Oh yes! the homes of England's clergy are

The fairest pattern we can emulate.

Our land would sadly fare without her Church,

Let noisy scoffers babble as they will.

God bless the Church of England, and preserve

Her sacred walls from insolent attack!

And, if her faults be great—take this to heart—

Let those that perfect are first mock at her.

Her virtues far outnumber them, and though

Ere long the owl may haunt her crumbling

    towers,

And poets wander through deserted aisles,

And strangers by her broken altars stand

To gaze upon her past magnificence;

More beautiful, more strong, in death than life,

She, like the fabled Phœnix, shall ascend

From her own ashes in renewèd strength.

My childhood flew by like a happy dream ;

Though Sorrow oft-times loitered at the gate,

It turned away as loth to enter there.

My playmate's home was mine, and mine was his

Of long descent, and proud historic name,

Nor he nor I felt difference of rank,

For children always are republicans.

Together on the hills we roamed, or else

We shared each other's different sports at home,

Or sometimes went amongst the villagers

With some small bounty for the suffering ;

Or conned our tasks together, for we had

The hours set for work as well as play.

Thus winged the time its rapid backward course,

Until he went to England's greatest school :

We met no more again for many years.

From time to time I heard how he advanced
In knowledge both of books and of the world.
Then that he left his college and took arms
(To serve his country, as the saying goes,
Though soldiers serve her less than other men).
Then that to wildest pleasures he was given;
But that which wronged him I would not believe.

My first great grief was when my mother died;
She who had watched me with such tender care;
And, looking on her thin and lifeless form,
I thought no lot was ever hard as mine.
So all of us in trouble do forget
To reckon up our many happy days;
When tempests howl, surrounding gloom per-
    vades:
It seems as if no sun had ever smiled.

The grave is but the gate by which the soul
Enters on everlasting bliss or woe.

Away, then, with those unbelieving moans,

Which equally for bad and good are made.

Away, too, with that funeral circumstance.

Which tells us not of hope, but dark despair.

Death must be grevious, for it tears away

Those who have twined themselves around our

      hearts;

Unfeeling would it be to scorn a tear :

But all the hideousness of funeral pomp

Speaks of annihilation, not of life,

And casts a slur on Christianity.

My nineteenth summer came, but ere it past

My father rested in the parish church,

Where he so long and faithfully had preached.

Four years had slow disease crept surely on;

While many heavy losses, and the thought—

When he was gone I should be destitute—

Hastened the sinking of his shattered frame;

My one stay died, and I was left alone.

'Tis said when Fortune frowns that friends
    grow cold ;
As if afraid the goddess might depart
From them, unless they bow to her caprice.
And so it is with many, but with those
Whom I accounted friends it was not so ;
For doors were opened, welcomes warmly given ;
Hard to refuse, but harder to accept :
For charity, however kindly given,
Destroys the pride of independency.

My story darkens when to earn my bread
I took a place as governess, and there
First felt the bitterness of servitude.
The lady was deemed Christian, for her name
Stood high on lists of numerous charities.
She had the Bible virtues all by heart,
And longed for the conversion of the world,
Which she helped forward by judicious pounds.
Donations gave to send two bishops forth

To bring some unknown tribes within the fold

('Tis said they showed a tendency to turn

Upon the hands like counterfeited coin;

But one would think that were impossible).

But let me hasten on, for every word

Now wrings my soul with speechless agony.

I had not long been there before I met

My early playmate, idol of my youth.

He spoke to me of those past happy times

When we together wandered on the hills,

Shared the same tasks, and tended the same

       flowers;

Of all the dear remembered haunts at home,

And named them one by one, as though he held

Their recollection with some fond delight,

And touched those chords which open lonely hearts.

For, like the exile, when he hears the strain

Of some sweet melody of early days,

Melts at the music waking thoughts of home,

And listens long in weeping happiness,

So I, so much alone, and desolate,

Looked to his coming as my only joy—

The sun that chased the clouds around my path.

No wonder that I loved him, for he was

Handsome, commanding, courteous, and kind,

And seemed with ease to conquer every heart.

But when my lady found he sought me out,

And talked with me both long and frequently,

Her righteous indignation roused itself:

" A governess ! a paid dependent ! dare

To aim at marriage with a noble's son,

Heir to a title and a vast domain,

When she four marriageable daughters had :

Such base ingratitude was never known !

Too long had she protected and sustained

A serpent in the bosom of her home ;

A mean usurper of her children's rights ! "—

She turned me out—then rung for evening prayers.

My lover—so I deemed him—followed me
With offers of assistance.   Then he spoke
Of his enduring love, of how he hoped
Ere long to call me by the name of wife.
From time to time he came, and then besought
That I would give him the last proof of love.
Few can resist when man a suppliant kneels:
Temptation swept across my soul—I fell.

Oh, that some kindly power would blot that page
From Memory's volume! or still "keen remorse,"
Or call that fatal moment back again!
A moment's error sometimes blasts a life.
Oh, then, reflect! and when fierce passions rage,
And wreak their violence upon the soul,
Remember that the Master's arm is strong—
That He has felt them, and can feel for us,
And, casting our own useless strength aside,
Lay them before the Lord in humble trust:
His arm shall shield us though we see it not.

Then he deserted me.   Strange though it seem,

I loved him then—must love him to the end.

A woman's love once given never dies.

But language has no power to portraiture

The changing moods of anger or despair,

That rent or strung my heart, or tell the depth,

The bitterness, of unavailing grief.

The knowledge what my future lot would be—

That I must live an outcast shunned by all—

As one to whom no mercy could be shown,

Had almost shaken Reason from her seat.

I recklessly frequented dens of sin,

Then deeply drank to drown my load of shame.

Yet in those haunts (of pleasure falsely called),

Where Luxury and Crime go hand in hand,

Are many of my sisters who can tell

A tale of misery as deep as mine;

Whose gentler natures never can be lost;

Who, when some passing thought of purer days

Has flashed across the mind like fire from God,

Have left with bursting hearts the laughing
     throng,

And in some silent chamber, on their knees,

Have prayed as none but broken hearts will pray ;

While rivers of repentance wet the cheek.

God hears those prayers, and turns a frown severe

On those who spurn such from society ;

For when the penitent looks round in hope

Some path will open for a virtuous life,

All doors are closed, and prudish Virtue sneers.

My tale is told.   A Christian lady came—

May Heaven's choicest blessings on her fall !

And led me to her pure and happy home,

From whence I go to a far-distant land

Where none will know my errors ; where, I trust,

Peace, if not happiness, may yet be mine.

MY PRAYER.

ALMIGHTY LORD, the Father of our race !
The Father of the good and bad the same ;
Oh! not in anger turn from me Thy face,
As in my lips I take Thy mighty name.
With penitence I own my sin and shame;
In wretchedness of heart before Thee bow :
Yet hopefully Thy soothing promise claim—
That sins like scarlet may bo white as snow.
Offended Lord, forgivo, and bless—yos, bloss—mo
    now !

When far from England's rocky shoro I dwoll,
My oxilo solf-imposod by past misdeods,
In mercy grant ono ray of peaco may fall
On my poor hoart, which now so soroly bloods ;
And as tho sonso of misory rocodos
Through healing timo, bo mino tho task to
    savo

Some erring sisters from that path which leads

So swiftly whence there can be no reprieve;

And bring them, like myself, Thy mercy to receive.

And, Lord, do Thou the hearts of all incline

To be more merciful to those who fall.

May they remember that the Great Divine

Encircled in His arms the worst of all.

When prone to harshly judge, may they recall

Their many sins observed by none but Thee;

Which, though their magnitude may seem but
    small,

Are often in Thy sight of deepest dye:

Bestow both Faith and Hope, but chiefly Charity.

And may Thy presence guard that noble band,

Which braves the coward's doubt, the cynic's
    sneer,

That it may stretch a loving, helping hand,

To check the outcast in her mad career!

The Master will to such be ever near

With His assistance and benignant smile :

Hear thy repentant daughter's prayer sincere ;

And as they labour, may there rise the while

"A virtuous populace in this my much-loved

isle !"

A VOICE FROM THE CONVENT.

"My hair is grey, but is not grey with age;"

My heart beats slowly, but 'tis not with time;

A prisoner, I pace my narrow cage,

Though these thin hands have ne'er been stained

    by crime.

Will no one burst these bars and set me free?

Ere my last hope, death or insanity!

                      F

When young and ignorant I took the veil,

Which was my thoughts from worldly things to sever;

Ten long, long years but yet they will assail

With wilder and more deadly force than ever.

Oh, some one burst these bars and set me free,

Ere my last hope, death or insanity!

I yearn to clasp some loved one to my breast,

To share his pleasures and to bear his woes;

The greater sacrifice the farther blest,

How woman can love woman only knows.

Will no one burst these bars and set me free?

Ere my last hope, death or insanity!

I long to join in childhood's merry game,

To hold a bonny boy upon my knee;

To hear him sweetly lisp his mother's name,

To soothe the simple griefs of infancy.

Oh, some one burst these bars and set me free,

Ere my last hope, death or insanity!

How sweet to rove the woods and fields, to hear
The wondering questions that my child would ask,
Or seat us in some shady nook, or fear
To see him eager on some climbing task !
Will no one burst these bars and set me free ?
Ere my last hope, death or insanity !

How sweet to listen to his faults confest,
To form his rosy lips in infant prayer !
'Tis deepest desolation and unrest,
No husband's and no offspring's love to share.
Oh, some one burst these bars and set me free,
Ere my last hope, death or insanity !

My life is one long penance, for those thoughts
Confession's cruel probing layeth bare ;
If these be sins, my hope of Heaven departs :
They cannot be, for God hath placed them there.
Will no one burst these bars and set me free,
Ere my last hope, death or insanity ?

No convent walls can shut out Nature's power—

Can keep affection from the human soul ;

That vow recalled, made in one fatal hour,

My life might yet some happy days enrol.

Oh, some one burst these bars and set me free,

Ere my last hope, death or insanity !

THE POET'S CONSOLATION.

ALL hail! to the heart-easing Goddess of Song,
So faithfully ever the bard's consolation;
Let doubtful ones pause ere they say it be wrong,
To kneel down before her in fond adoration.

When wanting a sixpence, I turn to my rhyme;
In pity my Muse will accede to my wishes:
The vision of poverty fades for a time,
And while the song lasts I am rolling in riches.

When out at the elbow, and out at the heel,
I list to her voice so soft and so winnin';

If she deign her presence, what wonder I feel
No wish for the finest of purple and linen?

When sorrow—when fears for my destiny press
    me—
When anxiousness broods like a cloud o'er the
    feeling,
My lovely one chases the doubts that distress me,
A work for mankind in the future revealing.

She speaks—and the words seem to soothe my
    pained brow—
" Oh, ne'er pen a line at which Purity blushes! "
With my heart wildly beating, I make her my vow,
And through me a torrent of ecstasy rushes.

May that resolution be always as strong,
As when I first made her my dutiful promise!
To me may my treasure for ever belong—
My riches, apparel, and unfailing solace.

HAPPINESS.

'Tis the penitent tear, redeeming the heart
From the dark-coloured stains which sin leaveth
    there,
A purity greater by far doth impart
Than that when no backslidings needed repair.

'Tis the penitent sigh, from the grief-laden breast,
That disperses before it the bitterest care;
Though fierce be the ordeal, 'tis for the best,
Like the African whirlwind that purgeth the air.

'Tis the penitent prayer assailing the throne,

In accents imperfect, heartbroken, unceasing,

Which turns to a smile Heaven's pitying frown ;

'Tis wrestling like Jacob that winneth the blessing.

What language can picture the feeling of bliss

When the sense of forgiveness steals over the soul ?

Beware tho' of testing that sense to excess,

For, too lightly treated, 'twill fly thy control.

'Tis the fond kiss of love on my mistress's cheek,

Each clasping the other in long, long embraces—

I'll try it again ere its taste I can speak—

Then tear, sigh, and prayer commence running
　　　races.

Methinks that above there be numbers of lovers—

The Master for Mary had strongest affection ;

The veriest child in the passion discovers

That where we feel most we are nearest perfection.

'Tis the exquisite thought that true pleasure
    affords,
When the mind boldly soars on the wings of
    Conception;
The treasures of poesy coins into words,
And casteth them earthwards for mankind's
    reception.

Or when Fancy stretches her numberless charms,
And lets me half catch some gem of expression,
I seize the enchantress, dispel her alarms,
And playfully hold her till perfect my lesson.

Men may talk as they please of their wine-bibbing
    mirth;
Let true love, religion, and poetry be mine—
Tho far sweetest joys we can taste upon earth:
All three lead to Heaven, all three are divine.

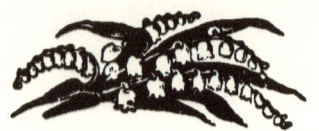

SOUTH AFRICAN SKETCHES.

THE JOURNEY OF THE TWO LEARNED
TUTORS.

Of all the joys o' human life,

I count the chief to be a wife:

Not one like Socrates' enchantress,

But a sweet, gracious, household goddess.

Of all the woes Fate may consign us,

I count the chief to be wife minus.

'Twixt these two poles there's much to please us,

And just as many ills to tease us.

No doubt that Woe was Weal's twin brother,

And came forth but to plague the other ;

And some events in all careers

Leave clearer marks than their compeers.

It is so, but the reason why

I leave to dull philosophy.

The motive of this hasty sermon,

My story's sequel may determine.

From Weston Town, then, it befell—

A sort of half-way house to hell,

Where drink and dullness rule the day,

Where beauty's seen but in decay,

Where nothing thrives but what will pay ;

Where people snarl at people's heels,

And kick or bite each champion feels ;

Where blacks and whites have separate churches

To follow their Divine researches,

And go to heaven or hell in factions,

According which best suits their actions ;

But here there is small room for blame,

In other places 'tis the same,—

Two learned tutors chanced to start

A journey in a two-mule cart ;

The one a deep and grave professor,

The other his profound successor.

Though young, their depth is reached by few ;

All said they knew " a thing or two."

The one could drink by hydrostatics,

The other carve by mathematics ;

Between 'em swear in full eight tongues,

And sing a hundred serious songs,

Knew all the mythologic failings,

But on their own spent no bewailings.

A deluge of the day before

Had soaked the roads three foot or more ;

To comfort them when falling weary,

On pilgrimage so wet and dreary,

Three well-filled flasks were stowèd handy—

For even learning likes its brandy :

Water for mixing was not heeded,

That lay upon the roads—when needed.

Crack! went the whip; jog! went the
     mules,

Jolting the wisdom of the schools;

Wide and more wide the water stretched,

The toll outside the town was reached;

The donkeys thought, 'twas time to rest,

For which, in Latin, they were blest,

And, lest they shouldn't understand it,

A Dutch translation well explained it.

     The town by distance soon looked small;

Shall wisdom's blessing on it fall?

The car was stopped, a solemn glass

Ensured for ever its success.

Betimes a mountain came in view:

Mentor remarked, " 'Twas very true

That mountains were the largest objects

Noticed in geologic pandects;

This one contains exhaustless wealth."
Mecœnas cried, "Then drink its health!"

There's much in Afric's wastes to please,
If mind and body be at ease;
If not, the fairest earthly scene
To grumbling vision seems but mean.
Its agèd flower the aloe shows,
The pretty blue-bell humbly blows,
North, south, east, west, ericas bloom,
The marigold grows by the broom;
Acacias, armed on every side,
Lift their round forms in despot pride.
His woolly charge the herdsman tends,
His carol with their bleating blends;
Seeks heathy pasture, which they share
With timorous antelope and hare.
The crafty jackal roams the plain,
The bustard tunes her shrill complain;

The secretary's loathsome prey
Hisses at times beside the way;
Gay tribes of songsters grace the scene,
Rousing the echoes in their spleen;
And on this day, fresh after storms,
The sun the face of Nature warms—
Like Beauty blushing at her charms.

Slowly they toiled through wet and slime,
The roads were bent on spiting Time;
The scent of flowers got in between
The puff of pipe or cigareen;
The lack of speed was borne with patience,
By notes of previous recreations;
Of gracious lassies left behind,
Of small flirtations called to mind.
Then future prospects.   One had done—
The other only just begun—
His duties.   Fervently they swore
Friendship and faith for evermore.

How many lasting bargains pass

Without that strong cement—a glass ?

A King and Kaiser after dinner

Hob-nob—and Peace will be the winner !

The freedom of ten millions may

Lie in a goblet of Tokay.

Hi ! There's a ditch with three feet water ;

The driver held the ribbons shorter.

The fall was steep, the farther side

Grimly the strength of springs defied :

The mules, by skilful tickling maddened,

Nearly upset the cart—but didn't.

A belt of trees now offered shade,

Both rested in the welcome glade.

Here comes one of the subject race !

A contrast he with the pale-face !

The brutish head, distorted limb,

Beyond a freak of nature seem.

And yet, 'tis said, that Bushmen claim
An origin with us the same
Though ages of debasement may
Have swept the stamp Divine away.
But to our friends, all but forgot.
They drank a professorial " tot "
To celebrate the famous spot.

The sun was waning on his round—
They still must traverse miles of ground ;
Wisdom got fired, the mules got tired,
Mentor Mecænas then desired
To sing a jolly roaring song,
To help or scare the mokes along.
When wine runs in, the wit runs out,—
The melody became a shout ;
The passers-by, with prescience dim,
Joined, thinking it must be a hymn.
The startled echoes spread the sound,
An eagle in his eyrie swooned—

Ten springboks died of palpitation —

Nine hares endured extravasation—

The mice, heart-broken, sought their
    holes.

In answer to their friends the moles,

They said, the noise concisely summing,

Building Societies were coming!

A napping owl a long breath drew

In deep disgust, and cried, " Tu-whoo !"

But even distance yields at last,

Though yards and miles be slowly past;

They went back some four miles, to find

A package they had dropped behind.

Nor wine, nor brandy, made 'em heady

At every glass they got more steady,

And only looked a little tired,

But proper as could be desired.

On ! on ! for it was falling dark ;

At last the watch-dog's welcome bark !

The hut-fires pierce the thickening gloom

Wo! the professors are at home,

To charm the company that evening

With converse moral and enlivening.

Well! Bishops are not free from fault,

And Methodists can do their malt.

The best of men have imperfections,

So leave our friends to their reflections.

We none of us so perfect are,

That Pharisaic pride should dare

To say, "I holier am than thou,"

Or flaunt the dec'logue on the brow;

But bear in mind in every case

If slapping Virtue in the face;

That Sin by Sorrow is pursued,

For Satan knows no gratitude.

THE EPILOGUE OF SPORT.

TO A SPRINGBOK BROUGHT DOWN BY THE RIFLE,

1864.

So this is Sport! Poor bleeding creature!

That agony in every feature,

May surely be the plaintive teacher

   From Mercy's throne!

To others let it prove the preacher;

   Not me alone.

That wondering eye from me decline!

So sore reproachful, yet benign;

To think that this is work of mine,

   Remorse doth quell me;

Poor thing! I'll join my tear with thine,

   Though that can't heal thee.

When thou this fatal day began,
None freer was on earth's wide span ;
That deadly messenger of man,
   An ounce of lead,
Has stretched thee on this barren pan,
   Thy life to shed.

Thy little one will call in vain ;
Its newly-nurtured strength will wane ;
Ere night, 'twill famish on this plain,
   Or else be caught ;
Two innocents caused wanton pain,
   In *manly* sport !

I'd rather now the gales caress
That graceful form, that light foot press
These heathy regions measureless,
   Where, at thy will ;
A miserable triumph this
   Of science' skill !

But thus we learn from hour to hour,

That every one who has the power

Delights to see the weaker cower,

    From some strange cause;

Maybe this is the strength and tower

    Of Nature's laws!

But looking higher, then I find

That He to all is just and kind;

The workings of that Mighty Mind

    Are always even;

How few to mercy are inclined

    On this side Heaven!

There! thou art gone! thy pain is past;

Though dumb and weakly, yet thou hast

A lesson taught me, which shall last

    Through my career;

In turn, I must the moral cast

    Both far and near.

I'll never more in sporting frame

Do such a tyrant deed of shame ;

Henceforth my chase be nobler game—

       The good of man ;

Full happy if I reach my aim

       In life's brief span.

———————

NOTES.

Note A.

`" Whose spire, the sentinel of centuries,
    Points, like the precepts old beneath it taught,
    Unerringly and calmly towards the skies."

I think it due to myself, as well as others, to say that these lines were written many years ago, forming part of a poem since destroyed. The idea, whatever it may be worth, is entirely my own. But, two or three weeks back, I took up a volume of Wordsworth's "Excursion," which I have never had the patience to travel through, and came by chance on the following line—

And spires, whose "silent finger points to Heaven."—
(*Excursion*, b. vi., ver. 19.)

Where the quotation comes from I know not; but as "Christmas Day" was ready for press at the time, I confess that the discovery of the above line gave me some uneasiness. I felt certain the critics would say that it was plagiarism. My three lines, though further developed, bear a strong resemblance to the one in Wordsworth. My first impulse was to re-write the verse, but, on second thoughts, decided to leave it ; because, as far as I am concerned, it is perfectly original. Hence this note. If it be decided against me after this explanation, let the three be put between inverted commas—I care not ;— but with even-handed justice let the following passages in Goldsmith's "Deserted Village" be put between inverted commas in every future edition.

GOLDSMITH.

" Remote from towns he ran his godly race,
   Nor e'er had changed, nor wished to change his place ;
   Unpractised he to fawn or seek for power,
   By doctrines fashioned to the varying hour.
   Far other aims his heart had learned to prize,
   More skilled to raise the wretched than to rise.
   *   *   *   *   *   *   *   *
   He chid their wanderings, but relieved their pain.
   *   *   *   *   *   *   *   *
   Allured to brighter worlds, and led the way."

CHAUCER.

" That Cristes gospel trewely wolde preche,
   His parishens devoutly wolde he teche.
   *   *   *   *   *   *   *   *
   But rather wolde he yeven out of doute,
   Unto his poure parishens aboute,
   Of his offring and eke of his substance.
   *   *   *   *   *   *   *   *
   This noble ensample to his shepe he yaf,
   That first he wrought, and afterward he taught.
   *   *   *   *   *   *   *   *
   He sette not his benefice to hire,
   And lette his shepe accombred in the mire,
   And ran unto London, unto Seint Poules,
   To seken him a chanterie for soules.
   *   *   *   *   *   *   *
   But dwelt at home and kepte wel his folde.
   *   *   *   *   *   *   *   *
   He was a shepherd and no mercenarie.

And tho' he holy were and vertuous,
He was to sinful men not dispitous,
Ne of his speche dangerous ne digne,
But in his teaching discreet and benigne.
To drawen folk to heven with fairnesse,
By good ensample was his besinesse.
* * * * * *
Him would he snibben sharply for the nones.
* * * * * * * *
But Cristes love and his apostles twelve
He taught, but first he fulwed it himselve."

One more instance :—

BURNS.

" It thirl'd the heart-strings thro' the breast."
" That gart my heart-strings tingle."

CAPERN.

" Make all the heart-strings tingle."

NOTE B.

No one can feel a more profound admiration for Robert
Burns than myself. I look upon him as the greatest poet
that ever lived; far above even glorious Shakespeare. His
like we shall never see again. He is, indeed, the pride of
Scotland. Scotland has produced, and is still producing, many
great men; but she will never see another Burns. With every
desire to speak well of this extraordinary man, I cannot con-
ceal from myself that many of his pieces have been the means
of anything but good. His " Scotch Drink " is a notable
instance. All the force of expression and the pungency of wit
are brought to bear for the purpose of making a degrading
habit appear less so. Why did not Burns show the other
side ? From carelessness, I suppose. That he saw the curse

of drink is evident from several passages in his poetry.   In
" The Author's Earnest Cry and Prayer" he speaks (it seems
to me), contemptuously—

> " Tell them whae hae the chief direction,
> Scotland an me's in great affliction,
> E'er sin they laid that curst restriction
> > > On aqua vitœ.
>
> *   *   *   *   *   *   *   *
>
> *   *   *   *   *   *   *   *
>
> But bring a Scotsman frae his hill,
> Clap in his cheek a Highland gill,
> Say, such is royal George's will,
> > > An' there's the foe.
> He has nae thought but how to kill
> > > Twa at a blow.
>
> Nae cauld, faint-hearted doubtings tease him :
> Death comes, wi' fearless eye he sees him ;
> Wi' bluidy han' a welcome gies him ;
> > > An' when he fa's,
> His latest draught of breathin' lea'es him
> > > In faint huzzas."

An under current of contempt is, I think, evident here, more
especially in the last. The poem which I have called " Strong
Drink " is an attempt to show the dark side of the question,
and dark it is. Let me observe, before I go further, that it has
been written in the first person solely to give it greater force ;
it must not be taken in any way as applying to myself.   The
motive has been that, if it should haply fall into the hands of
any one addicted to this fatal passion, it may apply more di-
rectly to his case.   Hence, I have put some of the truths in
the very strongest form of which I was capable.   I do hope
that it may be the means of making many, both young and
old, look at this easily-acquired vice in a true light; if that he

so, my aim will be accomplished. I have called drink England's curse; and so it is. I believe it to be the source of more than nine-tenths of our crime. Could I have put this more strongly in the poem, I would have done so; for this is no subject about which to mince matters. It is difficult, nay, perhaps impossible, to get at any result showing the exact connexion between drunkenness and crime; but all our judges, our magistrates, and our guardians of the poor, are unanimous in their testimony. Let me be allowed to give the following quotation from a well-known publication:—

"Drunkenness and its attendant evils seems to be keeping step for step with civilization. The time has long gone past when it was considered respectable to get drunk; but the time is apparently far distant when every one will consider it absolutely infamous to be even "half-seas over." Not that our friends the total abstainers are doing nothing. They have fought and are fighting a good fight, but against fearful odds. For instance, we learn from statistics recently issued, that in Ireland in the year 1869, 88,878 persons were charged before magistrates with being drunk or drunk and disorderly; the number is above 7 per cent. more than in the preceding year. The return shows also that in England and Wales in 1868, in a population of like number with that of Ireland, the number of persons charged with drunkenness (being drunk, or drunk and disorderly), was but 28,581, or not a third of the number charged in Ireland in 1869; but the comparison would have been less unfavourable for Ireland if it could have been made with the English return for 1869, for that return now issued shows in 1869 an increase of such charges over 1868 amounting to nearly 10 per cent. A comparison of the number convicted on charges of drunkenness in the two countries is more unfavourable for Ireland than a comparison of the numbers charged, as the rates of convictions to charges is greater in Ireland than in England. The numbers are these: In England and Wales in the year 1869 (year ending at Michaelmas) 122,310 persons were charged with drunkenness—89,859 men, and 32,451 women; and 93,638 were con-victed—72,869 men, and 20,769 women. In Ireland, with little more than a fourth of the population of England and Wales, there were in 1869, 88,878 persons charged with drunk-enness—72,408 men, and 16,470 women; and 78,693 were convicted—64,986 men, and 13,707 women. In both countries a much larger proportion of the women charged escaped con-viction than of the men; but that is no novelty. It would be difficult to show in figures the connexion between drunken-ness and crime; it is not done by a return which is annually made up, classifying the persons proceeded against for offences according to their known character. It is shown how many were known thieves, prostitutes, tramps, or suspected persons, and how many (that is, how many not already included under one or other of those four heads) were habitual drunkards? In England, in 1869, out of the 440,431 men, and 106,722 women proceeded against summarily or on indictment, only 26,445 men, and 9,233 women are thus classed as habitual drunkards; in Ireland only 8,894 men, and 2,105 women, out of the 201,426 men, and 43,965 women proceeded against. It would not be right to state the gross numbers proceeded against, without adding that the apprehensions for indictable offences were 29,278 in England and Wales, but only 600 in Ireland. It is the persons proceeded against summarily for minor offences, such as drunkenness, that swell the Irish list, the whole number proceeded against summarily being 517,875 in England and Wales, and as many as 239,390 in Ireland."

This does not represent the evil in half its magnitude. How many are there of whom we never hear—private drunkards—and of those whom perhaps we cannot call drunkards, but free drinkers? Have I, then, gone too far in saying—

" You've everywhere an institution
To breed theft, murder, prostitution,

> And spread abroad that destitution
>   Which you bewail;
> So then, by way of restitution,
>   You build a jail!"

Look at those hells upon earth—the gin-palaces! See how alarmingly they are on the increase. When will the Legislature discover that by giving every encouragement (not only security) to these places, where black ruin is dispensed at so much per glass, they are hastening the fall of that country which they profess so loudly to serve?

Be it observed that I would not cram teetotalism down any man's throat. I think liquors are given us to be used, as we use any other agreeable thing. The above remarks apply only to those who cannot take moderately—that go on "from fill to fill, from more to more"; and heaven knows there are many such! The only hope for them is—total abstinence. An habitual drinker said to me not long ago, "I do envy a man who can drink a glass of grog and then think no more about it"; to which I replied, "Then give it up." It was that remark of his which prompted the verse—

> "'Tis not for me, the social glass,
>   An hour with pipe and friend to pass," &c.

A word as to the stanza. Few of those who, like myself, are infatuated enough to clink rhymes, know its difficulty unless they have tried it fairly. The only English poem (that I remember at the moment of writing) in this stanza is Wordsworth's lament for Robert Burns. Burns used it freely, as all are aware. The use of the two languages "is very accommodating to him (Burns), who is able by this Scottish privilege to marry the most opposite and discordant rhymes." I must leave the reader to judge whether in "Strong Drink" the English language has altogether failed to adapt itself to the style of verse.

NOTE C.

> "There's, maybe, pleasure in the wine,
>   For when half drunk you're half divine;
> Song, Music, Painting—all the Nine
>   Are at your call."

This may appear far-fetched, but it is literally true. There are
some men who can hardly get out a dozen words when sober,
but when primed with a glass or two of toddy will talk
divinely. I was staying, some years ago, at a hotel in South
Africa, when I met with an instance of the kind. The gentleman (for gentleman he was) could not, or would not, converse when sober; but when half drunk, I never heard such a
talker! Erudition, refined criticism, wit, engineering, poetry
—nothing came amiss; and all in perfect taste. Burns seems
to have felt the same influence :—

> "O Whisky! Soul o' plays and pranks,
>   Accept a bardie's grateful thanks.
> When wanting thee, what tuneless cranks
>   Are my poor verses!
> Thou comes; they rattle i' their ranks."

NOTE D.

The greater part of the poem called "Rolando" was written
some years ago. This will account in some measure for the
imperfection in its design, and perhaps for a little extravagance
of expression here and there. It was my first effort in verse.
The origin of its title may be very simply explained. M.
Janfret's charming work, "The Travels of Rolando," was my
first prize, obtained, so says the writing on the fly-sheet, for
"diligence;" which, I believe, in schoolmistress's vocabulary,
means stupidity. This book made an impression on my mind
which will last through life. In giving a name to the indi-

vidual whose opinions are set forth in these lines, I thought
that of Rolando was peculiarly suitable. Whether he will
ever complete the tale of his wanderings, the writer knows
not. The intention was to take him through South America,
Palestine, and Italy; at present he has only reached America.
The slight sketch of the character of the American people
was not written at a moment's notice, but after long reflection.
It would have been impossible, in so short a limit as I have
allowed myself, to mark every virtue or every fault—the
prominent features only have been taken. I do not think any
keen observer will deny the truth of the following :—

> " The harmless decoration of a name,
> The homage which exalted titles claim—
> These are desired; now Wealth and Power unite
> To gild the structure, dazzle vulgar sight."

Will any one—even an American—deny it ? Where do
we find more extravagant homage paid to rank, merely as
such (unaccompanied by distinguished qualities, without
which rank is utterly contemptible), than in this wonderful
nation, except, perhaps, by virtuous dowagers in our own
happy land ? We in England are anything but faultless in
this respect, and I believe it results in America from old
habits or associations, not likely to be broken through for
many a year, in spite of their boasted democracy. It will be
long before all will discover

> " The rank is but the guinea's stamp,
> The man's the gowd for a' that."

It cannot be a good sign in any country that the highest
honour to which a citizen can aspire—making laws for the
good of his native land—should be thought so little of as it
confessedly is in America. That a seat in Parliament should
be avoided rather than sought after by those whose presence
would be most beneficial, cannot redound to the credit
either of the nation or the laws. In England a seat in the

council of the nation is esteemed a very high honour: long may it be so! But not so very far back in the history of our cousins anybody was fit to legislate. We cannot expect figs of thistles; so many of their statutes are anything but what they should be. Possibly the evil may now be correcting itself.

It has been said that the conquest of the South by the North clearly showed the stability of American institutions; that few other nations could have endured such a storm, much less have recovered so quickly from its violence. I do not think that there is much stability to be found. On the outside, it is true, they look firm enough, but I apprehend that the whole structure is too unwieldy to last very long. It is not my desire to appear in the character of a prophet; but my conviction is that American society will have its strength tried much more severely than it has had, even in the civil war. The following couplet was written five years ago, which I see no reason to alter:—

> " Until a despot rise, and with the sword
> Scourge, till a humbled nation own him lord. "

There are probably few who will not join with me in the tribute of admiring respect paid to the simple but noble Abraham Lincoln. His was a life which all might study with advantage. Sincere and unswerving, with a consciousness of his great mission, he could afford to despise those who looked at his horny hands and weather-beaten face instead of at his honest heart. Lincoln is one of the noblest names on the page of history. There has been but one other American who may be compared with him—George Washington; but Washington has derived much of his fame from being the ruler under whom independence was gained. Take that distinction away, and he must yield to his nobler successor. If I mistake not, the remembrance of "honest Abe" already holds a deeper place in the heart of the American nation than that of Washington. That he had all along the design of abolishing slavery, perhaps none who read his life will believe ;

in fact, there is evidence to the contrary; but neither did the first President know to what great events his course was leading him.

The statesman who shall be the means of abolishing the law of entail will confer a lasting benefit on his country. It requires no argument to show how injuriously this system works, because its results are staring us in the face. It has been calculated that there is land enough in the United Kingdom for the support of more than 120 millions of people; yet look at our pauperism, with about 40 millions. I give a quotation from a book which is not so much known as it deserves to be in spite of its many peculiarities: "Practical, Moral, and Political Economy," by T. R. Edmonds, B.A. "The United Kingdom of Britain and Ireland contains 74 millions of acres, of which at least 64 millions of acres may be considered capable of cultivation. Half an acre (with ordinary cultivation) is sufficient to supply an individual with corn, and one acre is sufficient to maintain a horse. Consequently the United Kingdom contains land enough for the sustenance of 120 millions of people and four millions of horses. We have, therefore, no reason to apprehend a real excess of population for many years. There may be an excess of population when compared with the quantity of food provided for it. It will be the duty of the British Government for many years to encourage agriculture, rather than to place checks on the increase of the population." It might be added, nor is it the duty of the British Government to drive them away, nor let them starve. Until there shall be one universal brotherhood of men, it is of little avail to say that they are as well in another country as here. Our invention, skill, and labour go to America, and are transformed by our rivals into a power which may at any time do us an injury. It seems to me the most unaccountable folly that the Government of this country should persistently drive away its own strength. Time will come when it may be necessary, but that time is yet far distant. The Americans, the Swiss, the Germans, can outvie

us in cheapness of manufactures—particularly the first-
mentioned. With the most suicidal policy, we are doing all
we can to transplant our industries to the other side of the
Atlantic. Not only that : look at the numbers of our starving
poor, able and willing to work, but who can find no work to do.
What is the consequence? Our gaols are filled; our expenditures
enormous, the numbers pressing on the bounds of subsistence
incalculable. Yet, while all this is before them, our statesmen
(if it be not a sarcasm to call them by that name) resolutely close
their eyes when pointed to its remedy. I have unfortunately
mislaid a pamphlet from which it was my intention to quote,
but, writing from memory, I shall not be far wrong in saying
that only about one six-hundredth part of the land of the
United Kingdom is free! (This I leave open to correction).
There is no need, then, to wonder at our thieves, paupers, and
pilgrims! Why has it not hitherto been abolished ? Because
the members of the House of Commons have been chosen, in
the main, from that class whose interests it is to uphold it.
It may be too much to expect from Britons the self-sacrifice
of the Greeks and Romans. We have not remarked it as yet,
although most of them have been forced in antiquarian hot-
houses. Out of charity, we will suppose that none of those
who hold entailed property have seen that such conditions
must of necessity be injurious to the interests of their country ;
and yet such a supposition carries with it an air of improbability
when we remember the many keen thinkers amongst the
members of the House of Commons. Now that the suffrage
is more justly distributed, it will be the people's own fault if
this glaring injustice is not speedily a thing of the past.

There are some very estimable but very timorous persons
who, whilst acknowledging the wrong of the law of entail,
would yet retain it, from some vague idea that its abolition
would soon do away with all the fine estates in the country.
With the characteristic haste of alarmists, they jump head-
long at a false conclusion, and, rather than run any risk whatever, would leave things just as they are. To state their idea

more clearly, they fancy that the whole of the United Kingdom must of necessity be immediately parcelled into farms and fields for cultivation, grazing, or something of that sort. Farewell then (say they) to all our pretty parks, plantations, and mansion grounds, the delight and astonishment of foreigners, and the pride of Englishmen! This objection—for as such it must be ranked, because held by a considerable number —has been unnoticed, as far as I am aware, by those who have written on the subject of entail, on account of its very simplicity. It is, however, entitled to respect, if only for its sincerity, and the veneration for whatever is marked by antiquity which it denotes, and which even the most ardent reformer feels.

In the hasty jottings of a "note" it would be impossible to refute this notion at any length; but the few following remarks in conclusion may not be out of place. There are many fine estates in England which, held by no entail, have nevertheless descended from generation to generation. Their owners have deemed it a point of honour to transmit them intact to their successors. Those successors have not, when young, for any length of time run to such excesses as would hopelessly involve them. They too have had a thought of those who should come after. Hence the absence of entail has been as great a security as entail itself, with this obvious advantage, that the exercise of restraint, economy, and foresight has been promoted with a beneficial effect on the character. Entail, on the other hand, is a premium on dishonesty and extravagance, and therefore an injustice. A man with strong passions is not very likely to exercise the virtue of self-restraint when he loses neither position nor property. The system is immoral, because it does away to a very large extent with the consequences which ought, in every well-regulated community, to follow the breach of those virtues which are considered the safeguard of that community. It is unjust, also, because all class privileges are unjust; and further, because while nominally the owner, he is not really so. What is a man's own

he can do as he likes with; but an entail owner cannot sell
what he calls his own. It is therefore not really his, but he
holds it as steward for heirs yet unborn. The owners of entailed estates must have felt this repeatedly. This brings us,
of course, at one bound to the conclusion that there must be
free trade in land. Any one must be able to sell to any one
who is able to buy. Yet those who advocate free trade in
iron, cloth, or any other commodity, oppose it in this case.
They shudder at the very idea. Free trade in land is what
England must come to, if she wish to retain her position
amongst the nations.

Let us see, then, whether it would result in the " parcelling "
spoken of. We will suppose the law of entail repealed to-
morrow, without any saving clauses, giving years of compen-
sation to the holders. A great deal of land would undoubtedly
come into the market; which for a short time would be
glutted, but would right itself more rapidly than any other
market. Necessity would be the supreme law, by which sale
would be regulated. The estates of bankrupt owners would be
purchased either by several small capitalists or by one large
capitalist. In the former case, it would be built upon or
cultivated to that extent; in the latter, the probability is in
favour of its remaining a private estate of the class first mentioned until some spendthrift put it under the hammer. It
would then gradually work into the hands of those who
undoubtedly have the only right; but the process would cover
about 500 years. As the population of Great Britain is now said
to double every seventy years, we will assume that the greater
stimulus given would double it in fifty years; then, taking the
effective male population as 4·44 of the entire population, and
making allowances for those in trade, those who emigrate, &c,
&c., the alarmists are endeavouring to bring the year A.D.
2400 or A.D. 2450 into the year A.D. 1871!! The grounds
of the calculation may be found at length on pp. 46—49 of the
work above quoted, to which I refer the readers of this note,
two pages being too much to transcribe here.

Note E.

It will be seen that I believe Dr. Livingstone to be no longer alive. Had he been, I feel sure he would have returned before this. I know something of the character of the country, having lived there nearly six years. No one will be more glad, but no one will be more surprised, to hear of his return than myself. A remark is necessary here to explain the tone of his address. People think very differently of him there from what they do in England—at least, as far as my experience goes. They cannot understand why he went out as a missionary, and then turned explorer. They acknowledge his perseverance, but see no hardship in his life ; the latter naturally, for almost any colonist would bear the same amount of fatigue. I do not think I am going too far in saying that he is anything but popular in the south of Africa. If Dr. Livingstone should turn up, I have made him say nothing that he need be ashamed of having uttered.

Note F.

In "Magdalen's Appeal" there has been no attempt at poetry ; it is a story put into a versified form, that is all. If it be the means of inducing any one person to think more charitably of the penitent numbers who so seldom meet with anything but scorn or contumely from those who themselves are not and cannot be faultless, the writer's purpose will be answered. If it be the means of inducing some to stretch a helping hand, or to give them a sisterly smile in place of the closed door and the black frown, the writer's expectations will be pleasurably surpassed.